DATE DUE

MAR 1 8 1999	SEP 2 0 2003
JUL 2 2 1999	NOV 1 9 2003
APR 2 1 2000	DEC 2 1 2003
DEC 8 2000	SEP 2 0 2004
JAN 0 5 2001	MAR 0 6 2006
MAY 2 1 2001	APR 0 5 2006
JUN 2 5 2001	JUL 2 1 2007
JUL 2 0 2001	MAR 2 1 2008
JUL 2 2 2001	JUL 1 9 2013
AUG 0 1 2001	
SEP 1 2 2001	
JAN 2 7 2003	

Clifford's
BIRTHDAY PARTY

NORMAN BRIDWELL

SCHOLASTIC
HARDCOVER

SCHOLASTIC INC.

New York

For Adam, James, and Patrick

Scholastic Inc. would like to thank the following contributors, whose generous support has made this commemorative edition possible. They join with Scholastic in wishing Reading Is Fundamental a glorious 25th Anniversary Year.

Norman Bridwell

R. R. Donnelley & Sons Company

Papyrus/Newton Falls and Lindenmeyr Paper Company

Penguin, U.S.A.

Buxton-Skinner Printing Company

Copyright © 1988 by Norman Bridwell.
All rights reserved. Published by Scholastic Inc.
SCHOLASTIC HARDCOVER is a registered trademark
of Scholastic Inc.

No part of this publication may be reproduced in whole or in part, or stored in a retrieval system, or transmitted in any form or by any means, electronic, mechanical, photocopying, recording, or otherwise, without written permission of the publisher. For information regarding permission, write to Scholastic Inc., 730 Broadway, New York, NY 10003.

Library of Congress Cataloging-in-Publication Data
Bridwell, Norman.
Clifford's birthday party / Norman Bridwell.
p.   cm.
Summary: Clifford, the big, lovable, red dog, celebrates his birthday.
ISBN 0-590-44232-5
[1. Birthdays—Fiction. 2. Parties—Fiction. 3. Dogs—Fiction.]
I. Title.
PZ7.B7633C1w 1991   90-9017
[E]—dc20   CIP
                                                                        AC

12 11 10 9 8 7 6 5 4 3 2 1   1 2 3 4 5 6/9
Printed in the U.S.A.   23

My name is Emily Elizabeth,
and this is my dog Clifford.
Last week was Clifford's birthday.
We invited his pals to a party.

Mom had ice cream and cookies.
We put up decorations.

When it was time for the party to begin,
nobody was there.
Where could they be?

We went looking for Clifford's pals.

They were all together at the playground.

I asked them why they hadn't come to the party.

Jenny said they wanted to come,
but they didn't have very good presents for Clifford —
not good enough for such a special friend.

I told them not to be silly.

Clifford would like whatever they got for him.

They all ran home to get their gifts...

and everyone came to the party.

First we opened the gift from Scott and his dog Susie.

Scott had blown it up as much as he could.

Clifford blew it up some more.

We really had a ball.

Then Clifford pulled out the stopper.

That was a mistake.

The next gift was from Sam and his dog Lenny.

It was a piñata!

We hung the piñata from a tree.

There were treats inside for all the dogs.

Clifford was supposed to break the piñata
with a stick.
He gave a couple of good swings...

and the piñata broke open.
The dogs liked the treats...

but we decided not to give Clifford any more piñatas.

We all laughed when we saw the gift from
Jenny and her dog Flip.
It was a little small for Clifford.

But it was just right for his nose.
Clifford hates having a cold nose.

Alisha and Nero's gift was a toy dog that talked.

Clifford thought it was cute.
He went to pet it.

Uh-oh.

They don't make toys the way they used to.

It was time for ice cream when Cynthia
and her dog Basker arrived.

They brought Clifford a gift certificate
from the Bow Wow Beauty Parlor.
He could get a free shampoo and haircut.

We each had our own idea of how Clifford might look after the beauty parlor.

I like Clifford just the way he is.
I thanked Cynthia for the gift,
but I slipped the certificate to Scott
and Susie. I knew she would like it.

Then came the cake. Clifford was surprised.
He was even more surprised...

when his family popped out!

He hadn't seen his mother and father
and sisters and brother for a long time.

Clifford liked the presents his friends gave him,
but having his family and friends with him
was the best birthday present of all.